Big Sister Tells Me That I'm Black

illustrated by Lorenzo Lynch

BIG SISTER TELLS ME
THAT I'M BLACK

Arnold Adoff

Holt, Rinehart and Winston New York

Library of Congress Cataloging in Publication Data

Adoff, Arnold.
  Big sister tells me that I'm Black.

  SUMMARY: A big sister helps her little black
brother realize his identity.
  [1. Afro-Americans—Poetry] I. Lynch, Lorenzo,
1932-   II. Title.
PZ8.3.A233Bi   811'.5'4   75-32249
ISBN 0-03-014546-5

For Brother Jaime
And   Sister Leigh

For All Their Brothers
            And Sisters

Grow Strong   Stand Free
                      A.A.

big sister tells me
    that i'm black
she says she knows me
    front and back

she says that tan and brown are black
        that tan and brown
        brown and tan
make big black woman
        big black man

she says that brown and tan are black
        and we are proud
           we shout out loud
hip   hip
        hip hooray
hip   hip
        i'm black today

hip   hip
       wish i may
who say
       black today

hip   hip
       wish i might
i   say
       black tonight

hip   hip
        hip hooray
black
        black
black to stay

big sisters says
    i'll be a man
she tells about
    our growing plan

she says that boys become young men
    that boy and girl
    girl and boy
grow big together
    big with joy

she says that boys become young men
and girls grow strong
to sing their song

that we are proud
we shout out loud

sis   sis
sis boombay
sis   sis
i'm grown today

sis   sis
        wish i may
who say
        grown today

sis   sis
        wish i might
i   say
        grown tonight

sis   sis
        sis boombay
grown
        grown
grown to stay

big sister tells me
        that i'm smart
she says she knows me
        stop and start

she says that both of us are smart
        that write and read
        read and write
make big smart woman
        big man bright

she says that both of us are smart
        and we are bright
            with all our might

        that we are strong
        to sing our song

        and we are proud
            we shout out loud

```
a      b
       c ok
a      b
       i'm smart today


a      b
       wish i may
who    say
       smart today


a      b
       wish i might
i      say
       smart tonight


a      b
       c ok
smart
       smart
smart to stay
```

big sister tells me
    that i'm black
she tries to keep me
    right on track

she says that black men must stand tall
      that man and woman
      woman and man
grow big black family
    big black plan

she says that black men must stand tall
      and we can see
        we must be free

that we are bright
with all our might

and we are strong
    to sing our song

that we are proud
we shout out loud

hip   hip
        hip hooray
hip   hip
        we black today

hip   hip
        wish i may
who   say
            black today

hip   hip
        wish i might
i   say
        black is right

hip   hip
        hip hooray
black
        black

we black to stay

THE AUTHOR

ARNOLD ADOFF is a poet and anthologist who taught for many years in Harlem and the Upper West Side of his native New York City. His poetry/picture books include *MA nDA LA, black is brown is tan, make a circle/keep us in: poems for a good day*, and *tornado: poems*. Among his poetry anthologies are *I Am the Darker Brother, Black out Loud, City in All Directions, It Is the Poem Singing into Your Eyes, The Poetry of Black America*, and *My Black Me*. Mr. Adoff lives in Yellow Springs, Ohio, with his wife, novelist Virginia Hamilton, and their two children, Leigh and Jaime.

THE ARTIST

LORENZO LYNCH, art director, artist and free-lance illustrator, is the author/artist of THE HOT DOG MAN and the illustrator of several other children's books. Mr. Lynch lives in Brooklyn, with his wife and five children.

THE BOOK

This book was set in Caledonia and Bookman typefaces.
The art was done with a felt tip pen and ink wash.